KIDS' COMPUTER FRIENDS

AT CAMP Icmi

Written By: Ashley Faye Behr
Illustrated By: George Karn

Daniel J. Behr Productions

DEDICATED TO ALL THE CHILDREN OF THE WORLD.

Publisher's Cataloging-in-Publication
(Provided by Quality Books, Inc.)

Behr, Ashley Faye.
    Kids' Computer Friends at Camp ICMI : written by Ashley Faye
Behr ; illustrated by George Karn.
    p. cm.
    SUMMARY: Berto goes to a summer camp where the counselors
are computers.

    1. Camping--Juvenile fiction. 2. Computers--Juvenile fiction.
I. Title.

PZ7.B45Ki 1997   [E]   0987654321
                      QBI97-41058   0100999897

Daniel J. Behr Productions gratefully acknowledges Jean Domke for graphic design,
Terry O'Neill for copy-editing, Kathy Quirk-Syvertsen for author's photo.

Published by DJ BEHR co.
211 Division Street, Box 707, Northfield, MN 55057
Tel: 612-435-7048   e-mail: djbehr@viakids.com
Visit our website @ www.viakids.com

Printed in the U.S.A.

The bright morning sun shone on Berto's face, awakening him; he knew it was going to be an exciting day. "What a neat dream!" he said to himself. "I'm going to go tell Mom!"

He quickly got dressed and went down to breakfast. He didn't have much time before he left for camp.

"Mom," he said, "I had the coolest dream last night! When I went to camp the counselors were computers! Wouldn't that be neat?"

"Oh, Berto, you sure have a great imagination!" said his mother. "Now you'd better get your bags. It's time to leave."

It seemed to take forever to get to camp because Berto was *so* excited. Finally they were there, Camp *ICMI* was before them!

Berto's mom walked him in, only to find his friend Rudy standing in the doorway. "Have fun at camp," his mom said, "and don't forget to e-mail me!" With that she left, after giving him a kiss on the cheek.

"Rudy, you'll never believe what I dreamed about last night. The counselors at camp were..."

"Excuse me," a voice interrupted. "I think you two are in my bunkhouse."

They turned around to see a computer talking to them!

"Please let me introduce myself. My name is WEB-E."

Rudy and Berto looked at each other in disbelief. "Y-you can talk!?" Rudy asked.

"Of course I can!" WEB-E replied. "I can walk too! Let me show you around camp."

Their first stop was the bunkhouse. Inside, they met two other boys. "I'm Akil," said one.

"And I'm Chen," said the other.

"I'm WEB-E, and this is Rudy and Berto."

Just then something whizzed by them and out the door. "Who was that?" asked Chen.

"That's ZiP-e," said WEB-E. "NET-E's younger brother. He's a junior counselor and he'll be in our bunkhouse. He's probably on his way to the computer lodge."

"Who's NET-E?" asked Akil.

"She's the girls' camp counselor," WEB-E replied. "Let's go and you can meet them both."

Once they arrived in the computer lodge WEB-E introduced the boys to NET-E and ZiP-e. "Wow, you can talk, too?" asked Rudy.

"Talk!" replied NET-E, "I can talk all day long. Do you have any questions about Camp *ICMI*?" she asked.

"I do," said Akil, "I know it's a computer camp, but what does *ICMI* stand for?"

"*I CAN MAKE IT!*" ZiP-e piped in.

NET-E continued, "The most important thing we learn here at Camp *ICMI* is that each one of you can make it and make a difference in our world!"

"C'mon," NET-E said motioning. "The girls should be finished unpacking, and we can go down to the lake for some swimming fun."

As they started walking, four girls already in their bathing suits approached the boys.

"There they are!" said NET-E.

"Hi, Berto," said Nailah.

"How do you know her?" asked Chen.

"Oh, she goes to my school," Berto replied.

"For those of you who don't know each other, this is Zita, Tomiko, Lizzie, and Nailah," said NET-E. "Girls, this is Berto, Chen, Rudy, and Akil."

"You boys hurry up and get changed. We'll meet you down by the lake," WEB-E said.

"Are you going swimming, too?" Rudy asked his new computer friends.

"No way!" said ZiP-e. "There are a lot of things computers can do, but swimming is *not* one of them. That would short-circuit us!"

Once they were all changed they met at the lake. The boys and girls were having so much fun they didn't realize it was almost dusk.

"Time to get out of the water and into dry clothes. We wouldn't want to miss the camp bonfire!" said NET-E.

"A bonfire!" shouted ZiP-e, "with hot dogs and marshmallows, *YAHOO!*"

They all rushed to change.

An hour later everybody was seated around the bonfire exchanging stories with E-Box, a talking mailbox.

"In the old days I didn't have a keyboard," he started. "I was and still am the happiest mailbox that ever..."

"Wow, look at how bright the moon looks tonight," Nailah noticed.

"That's not the moon!" Zita said. "That is!" she said, pointing.

"But then what is *that*?" Nailah questioned.

"Oh, that's BEAMER," E-Box answered. "Let me
tell you a little about BEAMER. BEAMER is a
giant satellite that allows you to send e-mail all
around the..."

"Doesn't he get lonely up there?" Lizzie asked.

"Oh no. Other satellites and the stars keep him
company. Did you know that each one of the stars
is like each of you? No two are the same, and
each one is full of hope and beauty."

"Look! A big bug just buzzed past!" Tomiko exclaimed.

"Did it have a net?" ZiP-e chimed in.

"I-I think so." she answered hesitantly.

"Then it must be Bug'n, she's out catching fireflies, I hear she has a surprise for you!" ZiP-e added.

"Is that her job here at camp?" Lizzie asked.

"Yes, for fun, but her real job is keeping the computers bug-free." answered WEB-E.

It had been a long and exciting day for all of
them, so ZiP-e and the campers headed up to the
bunkhouses, while NET-E, WEB-E, and E-Box safely
put out the fire.

As each camper crawled into bed, they discovered
a natural nite-lite, a jar of glowing fireflies.

The campers awoke the next morning to find
a note on each of the bedside tables which read,

With that the children let the fireflies go, ate a healthy breakfast at the mess hall, and continued on to the computer lodge.

"What would you like to learn today?" NET-E asked.

"I'd like to learn about e-mail," Zita said.

Just then the door popped open and in flew the cutest little envelope.

"Who better to help us with our e-mail needs than our e-mail expert, E-Mme!" NET-E announced.

"I suppose she can talk, too!" Lizzie stated.

"I sure can, in almost every language of the world!" E-Mme said confidently.

"You can? Wow!" said Zita. "Do you think you could help me with my Spanish? I'd love to have a pen pal from Peru. My Grandfather is from Peru," she declared proudly.

"Si, Señorita!" E-Mme returned.

"How about Kenya?" asked Akil.
"Or Hong Kong!" exclaimed Chen.
"Great ideas. Let's get started." E-Mme said.

After the kids were finished with their letters, E-Mme flew out the door just as quickly as she had flown in.

"Where did she go?" asked Berto.

"She's off to deliver your e-mail," answered NET-E.

"Will she get it delivered before we leave camp?" asked Tomiko.

"She'll get it there and be back before you can say baseball!" exclaimed ZiP-e.

"Baseball!" shouted WEB-E. "I love baseball! Hooray!"

As the campers shut down their computers and were running out to play, NET-E called to ZiP-e and WEB-E, "Don't forget to push in your keyboards!"

The next few days were full of baseball and swimming, cookouts, campfires, and computer fun, and as the campers headed home Berto thought to himself, "It's amazing what can happen if you dare to dream!"